XTREME MYSTERIES

#2. CROSSED TRACKS

Laban Hill

XTREME MYSTERIES

#2 CROSSED TRACKS

Laban Hill

HYPERION PAPERBACKS FOR CHILDREN

NEW YORK

XTREME
MYSTERIES

#2. CROSSED TRACKS

Laban Hill

"Eat dirt!" Natalie Whittemore yelled over her shoulder as she powered down a rocky trail on her mountain bike. She bounced off a tree root and sailed across a dip in the trail.

"Yum!" her friend Kevin Schultz replied. Following close behind Nat, he cranked over the root and landed hard in the dip.

Bzzzzz! Wall Evans, another thirteen-year-old classmate, rubbed his front wheel against Kevin's rear wheel.

Jamil Smith pumped frantically, trying to keep up with his more experienced friends. This was Jamil's first time off-road, and he felt totally out of control.

Nat, Kevin, and Jamil had been tight since kindergarten, and were all extreme-sports freaks. They'd just met Wall a month ago, but he was fast becoming one of the crew.

"This way!" Nat turned down a steep access road of

Hoke Valley Ski Resort. Her bike flew across a gravel wash. "Power through it!" she directed as she led her friends along the first part of the trail that would be next weekend's Bear Claw Mountain Bike Race. The course was five kilometers long. Three and a half ran through the back trails of Hoke Valley Ski Resort, while the last kilometer and a half snaked down an old public access trail and turned onto a flat dirt road for the final sprint.

Nat bounced down the rocky hill like a pinball. Her bike was a red blur. She shifted into a higher gear and pedaled harder. She splashed dead center through a wide mud puddle and left a big wake behind her.

"This is insane!" Jamil screamed from the back of the pack. He tried to control his bike on the steep hill covered with loose gravel. His fat rear tire slid left and he braced for a hard fall.

"Miracle!" Jamil huffed as he managed to stay on his bike. He sucked air and closed his eyes as he pumped harder. At twelve, he was a year younger than Nat, Wall, and Kevin, but in most sports he was their equal. On a snowboard he was the guru of the valley. With off-road mountain biking, though, he was struggling.

Nat was setting a wild pace, but that was no surprise. She was a mountain biking maniac, and she was in her favorite spot—the lead.

Nat headed for the steeply banked turn that led to a threadlike singletrack, up about two hundred feet. Kevin was right behind her, matching her pedal stroke for pedal stroke. Kevin was one of those amazing natural athletes.

No matter what sport he tried, he always seemed to master it. Of course, it helped that he always had top-of-the-line equipment: his parents owned a sports shop in Hoke Valley.

Jamil was dropping farther and farther behind, his eyes locked on the mud lake his bike was intent on hitting sideways. Mud splashed onto his face. Afraid he would slip, he raised himself off the bike seat, cranked his pedals to a position parallel to the ground, and concentrated on keeping his body over his fat tires.

The mud wrapped itself around Jamil's tires and locked them in place. The bike shuddered to a sudden stop.

"Whoa!" Jamil screamed as he did an endo. "Mayday! Mayday! Crash landing!" He did a quick shoulder roll into the sticky goop.

Thuck! The mud slurped as Jamil sat up. His house key, which was on the end of a chain around his neck, was plastered against his cheek. His legs were twisted up in his bike. His green "Skate till Death" T-shirt and baggy black shorts were smeared with mud.

The rest of the crew circled back.

"I told you to pedal *through* the mud," Nat said, laughing. She pointed to the spot on Jamil's face where the key was glued.

Jamil put his hand on his cheek and found the house key. "I thought you meant pedal going down the hill."

"On that hill?" Kevin responded. "You got to be kidding. Ride your brake, dude."

"Well, don't just stand there," Jamil said. "Help me out, man."

"I'm not getting smeared with gross mud," Nat cracked.

"Too late," Wall said. "You should see your back."

A spray of mud spread up the back of Nat's bright blue and red patterned bike shirt.

Jamil dragged his bike to the dry part of the double-track. "I don't think I'm cut out for this mountain bike stuff." He began to wipe off the globs of mud that clogged his brakes. Jamil felt more at home with his feet strapped to his snowboard, shredding down the slopes on clean, cold snow. But Nat, a rabid off-road mountain biker, had convinced him to give biking a try.

Nat reached over and grabbed Jamil's water bottle and squeezed out a stream over his gears. "You'll get the hang of it by the first race this season," Nat said. "We've got a whole week to practice."

"And besides, you have the wrong tires," Kevin observed.

Jamil looked at his fat, knobby tires. "I thought these were mountain bike tires."

"They are," Kevin answered, "but they're not for mud or loose gravel. They're hard pack tires. These are mud tires." Kevin pointed to his tires, which were knobby only on the sides, and thinner.

Jamil looked longingly at Kevin's steel-frame F1000 bike with tough front fork shocks, totally awesome grip shift, and clipless pedals. Jamil's mountain bike was a hand-me-down from his dad. It was practically Jurassic in comparison even though it was only four years old. Every year, bike technology was totally revolutionized by some new breakthrough, making last year's model ready for the scrap heap.

"Hey, someone's coming down the trail." Wall turned toward the sound of tires crunching gravel.

"It's Phil," groaned Nat. Phil Speck and his two buds, Max Resnik and Joe Iannuzo, were at the top of the hill that Nat and her friends just came down. "I bet he'll complain about something." She unbuckled her helmet and tossed it on the ground. A tangle of long blond hair fell down her back.

"Yo, yo, yo," Phil called when he hit the mud puddle. He shifted into low gear and cleared the puddle effort-lessly. "I thought you were prepping the course for next weekend."

"I am," Nat replied.

Phil dabbed with his left foot and came to a stop. "Well, the trail is a bust so far. It's rutted and sections look like they'll wash out with the next rain."

"I almost blew a tire on a ski pole someone had thrown across the trail," Max added.

"The race isn't for a week," Nat said. "And we're right in the middle of mud season. Everything will be ready on time."

"I hope so," Phil said. "It's kind of a big job for you to handle, isn't it?" Phil had prepared the Bear Claw Mountain Bike Race course for the last two years. He couldn't do it this year because he had his senior high school project to finish. When the competition committee selected Nat to direct the prepping, Phil protested that she was too young, too inexperienced.

"Not enough climbs and too much singletrack in this course," Joe remarked, teasing Nat. "You should have let somebody else do it."

"Are you bent? This course is amped all the way," Kevin piped up to defend Nat.

"I don't know. This isn't a Bear Claw, it's a Sunday stroll," Phil replied.

"What?" Nat said, surprised. "You've been dogging me about the course since the committee chose me last fall. What do you think should be done?"

"The race should start at the top of Mount Olley," Phil insisted. "Then snake down toward town."

"The Bear Claw is a cross-country race, not a down-hill," Nat argued.

"Whatever," Phil said as he climbed back onto his saddle and pedaled on. Max and Joe followed close behind.

"Thanks for the tips," Nat called after them. "I'll keep them in mind." She picked up her helmet. "Like never," she muttered.

"Don't sweat it," Kevin reassured Nat.

"I can't help it," Nat admitted. "He's the expert and I'm taking his job." Nat ratcheted her pedals backward in frustration. "I don't think I can cut it."

"He's just jealous because he can't do it," Kevin said.

"Let's ride," Jamil suggested. "I was thinking . . . maybe I should do the cyclocross race. At least I'd be off my bike some of the time." He scraped mud off the bottom of his shoe.

"Yeah, off your bike and running uphill with it on your back," Nat snorted. "That's your kind of race." She pushed a strand of hair out of her face and tucked it back under her helmet.

Jamil shook his head. Tufts of his short, blond dreads stuck out of his helmet like crabgrass. He hopped back onto his bike without another word and rode about a hundred feet.

"Wait!" Nat called to him. "Look at the mess you made." She was pointing to the mud puddle.

"How can a mud puddle be messed up?" Jamil asked. "It's mud. It's already a mess."

Nat gave Jamil a withering look and laid her bike on the edge of the trail. "The matter is that you left a huge rut." She waded into the mud. "This is just the kind of stuff Phil's giving me grief about."

"You sound just like my mother," Jamil replied and rode back.

Nat ignored his comment. "When the mud dries, there will be this big rut in the middle of it." She stomped the rut down and smoothed out the mud with her feet. "The next time it rains, the water will flow like a river through it and begin to erode the trail."

"Oh, I get it," Jamil replied. "And the trail will be a real pain to ride on."

"Right," Nat confirmed. "And by the time of the race in a week, nobody'll be able to stay on the trail."

Jamil hopped on his bike and rode ahead. "I didn't expect mountain biking to be like school."

Nat stuck out her tongue at Jamil's back. "I just want this race to run perfectly. It's the first time I've had this kind of job, and I don't want to mess it up. Mr. Clary might never let me again." Nick Clary, Bear Claw's president and Nat's science teacher at Hoke Valley Middle School, had been Nat's biggest supporter for the job.

"You're doing great," Wall encouraged.

"Yeah, that's why Phil's trying to get the course changed," Nat groaned.

"Don't sweat Phil," Kevin said. "He's a hard case, but you've got to let his bad vibes roll off you."

"You've got the maps for the race already printed, and all we have to do is clean up after the winter," Wall added.

Jamil circled back and added his two cents. "Don't be such a perfectionist. So what if the mud puddles dry with ruts?"

"It just makes for a more exciting race. And exciting is what we want," Wall said, "especially since Saturday is Kevin's birthday, and he's got to have some kind of thrill to balance out the disappointment of losing to me." Wall thumped his chest with his fist.

"In your dreams," Kevin shot back.

The four of them rode on, each leaning over their handlebars as they pumped. The trail was a wide doubletrack here, but the singletrack section of the course was just ahead.

"Come on, grandma," Jamil called from out front. "You're slowing us down."

"I'll show you slow," Nat said. She stood on her bike and cranked her pedals hard. She easily shot to the lead.

By then, Jamil was huffing. "I don't get it," he shouted at her. "You're not in better shape than me. Why aren't you tired?"

"It's my secret formula," Nat replied as she sucked down a drink from her water bottle.

"No, really," Jamil persisted. "What am I doing wrong?" He pedaled furiously trying to keep up with his friends.

"Try switching to a harder gear," Kevin suggested as he whipped by Jamil. "You're wasting energy by doing so many revolutions."

Jamil shifted up. "But this is hard," he complained.

"It'll get easier as you get used to it," Wall reassured Jamil.

Kevin came up beside Nat. "Race you to the end."

"Start sucking dirt, 'cause all you're going to see is my back tire," Nat shouted. She powered in front of Kevin and hit the steeply banked, off-camber turn that led onto the singletrack full bore. She had to fight her bike to stay on the trail. The singletrack was used in the winter as a cross-country ski trail.

Nat wove through a technical part where the single-track made several sharp cutbacks going downhill. Then she looked over her shoulder and stuck her tongue out at Kevin.

Bad move!

Nat's tire plowed into a massive tree trunk lying across the trail. She brutally endoed to a perfect face plant in a mud puddle.

"Whoa!" Kevin screamed as his bike tangled up with Nat's.

"Pile up!" Wall yelled as he and Jamil quickly dabbed to a stop.

In a flash, Jamil was off his bike. He hurdled the wide tree trunk blocking the trail and dashed to Nat's side. "You need a pilot's license to fly like that."

"And a parachute!" Kevin added. Kevin reached over the log and extended his hand.

"I'm fine," Nat said. She waved off Kevin's hand. "I don't need any help." She sat up and tried to stand.

"Oooh, woman of steel," Jamil cracked.

Drops of blood pooled on the hand that Nat used to steady herself. Startled, she sat back down.

"Are you all right?" Wall asked, concerned.

"Medical emergency. Nat's brain is oozing out of her skull," Jamil announced like he was talking into a walkie-talkie. "Call in helicopter rescue. We're going to need a Med Evac."

"You're just the guy I'd want around in a *real* emergency, Jamil," Nat said. "I'm fine, fortunately."

"Here, I've got some gum," Jamil said, pulling a piece out of his mouth. "This should stop the bleeding."

"Gross," Nat said. "Give me my first-aid kit." She brought her hand to her forehead and examined the blood on her fingers. "It's not bad."

Kevin hopped onto the tree trunk and walked it to the end.

Jamil held his hand in front of Nat's face and quickly flashed different combinations of fingers before her. "How many fingers am I holding up?" Even though Nat and Jamil were always busting each other, they were best friends.

Wall unzipped the pouch attached to the underside of Nat's bike seat. A small blue box with a red cross on it spilled out along with a smaller black case. Wall tossed the blue box to Jamil.

"What's this?" Wall held up the small black case.

"Repair kit," Nat explained. "I can fix just about anything from a broken chain to a flat tire on the trail."

Jamil squirted a little antibacterial cream on a bandage. "Why would you need all that?"

"Would you rather carry your bike out of the woods or ride it?" Nat asked.

"I get it," Jamil said as he put the bandage over Nat's cut. "Good as new. How's your neck."

Nat automatically rubbed it. "It's fine." A few weeks

earlier she had crashed and landed on her neck when the Spring carnival's Big Air event was sabotaged. With Wall's help, they had nabbed the culprit.

"We got to clear this tree," Nat said as she hopped up. "It's blocking the Bear Claw."

"Hey!" Kevin called. "Look at this." He was standing at the base of the tree trunk.

"Looks like someone cut it down," Jamil observed.

"And recently," Wall added. "I can still smell the burn marks from the chainsaw." Wall always noticed unusual clues like that.

Nat glanced up through the canopy of the forest at the sky. "It rained yesterday, but not today," she considered as she rubbed her hand in a pile of sawdust. "This sawdust is dry."

"So it was cut today." Kevin finished Nat's thought.

"But why?" Wall asked as he knelt beside the trunk. "Pine's not any good for firewood. And there's no logging going on around here."

"I can't believe someone would be so thoughtless," Nat said. She kicked the tree trunk. "Ouch!" She grabbed her toe.

"Hey, klutz, need the first-aid kit?" Jamil smirked.

"Ha, ha," Nat replied.

"Maybe someone wasn't so thoughtless," Wall suggested.

"You mean what if the tree was cut down on purpose?" Nat said. "That would be just my luck." She rubbed the bandage on her forehead.

"Of course it was cut down on purpose," Kevin said. "The person carried a chainsaw all the way into the woods and cut the tree down. That's not done accidentally."

"No," Nat said. "That's not what I mean." She shook her head impatiently. "What if the person who cut down the tree did it to block the Bear Claw? You know we've gotten a lot of static from hikers and environmentalists. They think mountain biking tears up the woods."

"But they wouldn't destroy the woods to stop us," Kevin replied.

"Well, then," Nat countered. "What about someone who doesn't want the Bear Claw to take this trail?"

"You mean like Phil?" Jamil blurted.

"Why not?" Nat shrugged.

"I don't think Phil would do that. Maybe he's jealous, but he wouldn't put the race in danger," Kevin replied. "Or would he?"

"Even if he didn't do it, you know we're going to get grief for it," Nat said. "Once the hikers find this tree, we're doomed. They've already got us banned from national forest trails and most state forest trails, too."

"I think we've got a mystery that needs solving," Kevin concluded.

"No," Nat countered. "We've got a tree that needs moving."

"Well, now I can't do either. I got to get back," Kevin said. "My parents need my help with the sport climbing class tonight." This spring Kevin's dad had built an indoor climbing wall in their store.

14

"We got to move this tree first," Nat insisted. "That's why we're out here, to clean up the trail. Remember?"

"You and what bulldozer?" Jamil cracked.

"We can push it aside if we do it together," Nat said.

"Not now," Wall replied. "I've got to go work on a logo design for a contest."

"All right," Nat said with an edge of disappointment. "But promise to help me tomorrow."

They nodded, knowing that it was no use telling Nat that clearing the trail wasn't their idea of fun. Nat was an enthusiastic joiner and organizer who loved to volunteer herself—and her friends—for all sorts of activities.

"Yes, Mom," Jamil cracked.

Nat tried to give him a sharp look, but burst into laughter instead.

"We're going to have to find out who did this," Kevin explained, "so we don't get blamed."

Nat nodded. She liked a mystery as much as Jamil, Kevin, and Wall. She just wished it wasn't happening here and now. The Bear Claw was going to be enough work without this sort of strange thing interfering.

They lifted their bikes over the trunk and rode the last kilometer of the course. The trail was littered with branches and leaves. While her friends rode ahead, Nat periodically stopped and cleaned the trail. As she worked, her mind drifted back to the fallen tree. It really disturbed her that someone would block the trail like that. Something so obvious couldn't have been an accident.

But who would block the trail?

15

Only one name kept popping up. Phil. He wanted the Bear Claw to go in a different direction. He was definitely not happy that Nat had been picked to prep the course.

Or am I being paranoid? she wondered.

An hour later, Nat was sitting at the kitchen table in her family's apartment above the Bookworm, a bookstore her parents owned. She had the map of the Bear Claw spread out on the table, and she was marking the spots that she had to clean up the next day.

A slight tickle suddenly shivered behind Nat's right ear. She reached up and scratched. Then, a ticklish sensation started behind her left ear. She swatted the air, thinking it was a fly.

For a minute, the fly seemed to disappear and Nat became engrossed in her map again. Then an exposed part of her neck tensed. A shiver went down her spine and she spun around to see what it was.

"MOM!" Nat yelled. "She's at it again!"

Standing about four feet behind Nat was her little sister, Ella, who was holding a thin wire with a feather attached to it. "Whaaa?"

"MOM!"

Wendy Whittemore climbed the stairs into the kitchen. "What did I tell you two?" she demanded from the kitchen doorway. "Nat, aren't you a little old to be calling me into your arguments with Ella?"

Ella waved her feather in Nat's face. "I'm not touch-

16

ing you!" she protested.

"Mom, you know she won't leave me alone if you don't give her a direct order," Nat complained.

The feather floated in her face again.

Nat grabbed it and yanked the wire out of Ella's hand.

"Hey!" Ella cried. "That's my science experiment."

"Do I have to send both of you to your room?" Mrs. Whittemore asked.

"Oh, no," Nat groaned. "Send me anywhere but the same room as her."

Nat hated having to share her room with her sister, Ella, but her parents wanted to live above the store and it was only a two-bedroom apartment. The one good thing about living with a messy little sister is that Nat had learned to be super-neat and super-organized. But she hadn't yet learned to be patient with Ella when she played these annoying games.

Nat threw the wire and feather at Ella's feet. "I'm hungry. What's for supper?"

Mrs. Whittemore went to the fridge. "I've got some chicken pot pies I can stick in the microwave." Mrs. Whittemore was not a cook. If she had any free time, she was always writing poetry in her notebook or poring over the latest edition of poetry to come in the store. Their dad, Jake Whittemore, was the cook in the family.

This evening, however, the Bookworm was unexpectedly busy, so Mr. Whittemore couldn't sneak upstairs and prepare dinner. On nights like these, the Whittemores either ate leftovers or pot pies from the freezer.

"Sounds good," Nat responded, glad to change the subject. She couldn't care less what she ate as long as it filled her up. In this way she was more like her mom than her dad.

Nat closed her books to make room for the silverware and placemats.

"How're the race preparations going?" Mrs. Whittemore asked as she placed the pot pies into the microwave.

"I wish I could help," Ella whined.

"Maybe someday," Mrs. Whittemore replied. "This is Natalie's job, and she had to work hard to get it."

"Maybe never," Nat muttered. Out loud she said, "The ride went well today until I ran right smack into a huge pine tree lying across the trail."

"Oh," Mrs. Whittemore said. She came over and examined Nat's forehead. "Are you all right, honey? I didn't realize that cut was from a fall."

Nat shook her head. "I'm okay, really. It's just a cut. My toe hurts a lot more than my head." She pulled off her shoe and sock and examined the purplish bruise on the end of her big toe. "I was brilliant enough to kick the tree after I ran into it. This tree is going to be hard to move. We're going to meet first thing tomorrow to take care of it."

"You talking about the Bear Claw?" Mr. Whittemore asked as he came into the kitchen. "Tell me about the prep work."

Nat explained how she and her friends had cleared the trail and smoothed out the mud puddles.

"Sounds like you're doing terrific work," Mr. Whittemore said.

"Thanks." Nat smiled. "But most important is that I'm going to leave Kevin in the dust come next Saturday's race." Nat and her friends were competitive with each other, but Nat especially liked beating Kevin, who was a tough opponent in any sport.

Just as Mrs. Whittemore set the pot pies on the table, the phone rang.

Nat jumped up, but Ella beat her to it.

"It's for you. It's Mr. Clary," Ella said.

"It's still dark!" Jamil complained as he watched Nat ride up. They had agreed to meet early Sunday morning at Hoke Valley Ski Resort's lodge.

"Aren't we cranky this morning," Nat said as she skidded to a stop. "The sun is just blocked by Mount Olley. It'll be over it in a minute."

"I'm cold." Wall was sitting on the steps sipping a cup of hot chocolate next to Kevin. His hands were wrapped tightly around the cup. Jamil had made everyone hot chocolate in the lodge's kitchen. Even though the resort was closed for the season, Jamil had access to everything since his dad ran the place.

"What's up?" Kevin said to Nat.

"Mega-bad, bad as bad and badder," Nat replied. "Mr. Clary called me last night."

"Oh, no," Kevin moaned.

"Yeah," Nat said. "And he said I'm going to be yanked from my job if the course is as bad as Phil said it was."

"Phil called Mr. Clary?" Jamil blurted.

Nat dug her toe in the dirt. "He told Mr. Clary Joe Iannuzo broke ten spokes on a tree limb that wasn't cleared. And he complained about the pine tree lying across the trail."

"What else did Mr. Clary say?" Jamil asked.

"Nothing much," Nat replied. "I just promised him that everything is under control and that we're moving that tree this morning." Nat straddled her bike. "I just hope you guys are ready."

"I won't be ready for another two hours," Jamil groaned. "But if we got to go, we got to go."

As they rode off, the sun peeked over the ridge, sweeping a warm blanket of sunlight on the valley. It promised to be a warm spring day by afternoon, but that was hours away. Right now, it was still chilly, and in some places the early morning frost hadn't even melted.

The crew crunched through the meadow grass to the start of the course.

"Let's move it!" Nat shouted over her shoulder as she powered through a couple of tight switchbacks and climbed a gravel-covered incline.

They hit the same killer, banked, off-camber turn that led into the singletrack as yesterday.

Nat's tires slid sideways. She dabbed her right foot and muscled her bike back under her body.

"Nice recovery!" Kevin called.

As they reached the technical section of the single-track, Nat stood off her seat and used her legs like shocks to absorb the bumps. Then she sat back on her bike to stabilize her rear tire. She didn't want to slide on the slick, tight turns as she rolled quickly downhill. She kept her eyes focused ahead so she'd be ready to pull up when she came to the pine.

"Watch out!" Jamil yelled. He had lost control on the steep hill and was fighting his bike to stay on the trail. He missed a quick cutback as his front tire biffed into a fat root. The root pushed his bike sideways. He kissed an aspen with the side of the tire about a yard off the trail and slammed against the ground.

"Ow!" Jamil grunted. He sat up and looked at his elbow, which was throbbing in pain.

"Trail rash," Nat explained when she saw the bloody scrape on his elbow. "Happens all the time." She ratcheted her pedals backward to keep her balance on her bike without dabbing her foot on the ground.

"For you, Jamil, the trees off the trail are just as dangerous as the ones across the trail," Wall cracked. He reached out a hand and helped Jamil up.

They rode the last hundred yards to the fallen pine tree.

Nat hopped off her bike and climbed on the trunk blocking the trail.

"Do you really think it was done on purpose?" Jamil asked. He pulled off a piece of bark. Sticky sap covered his fingers. "Hey, fresh pine scent. That's the smell of our bathrooms at school." He waved his fingers in front of Kevin's face.

Kevin wrinkled his nose. "Modern civilization has evolved so much that no matter where we go, we're reminded of a toilet."

"This has to have been done on purpose," Nat persisted, ignoring Kevin's joke. "And I think Phil is behind this. He must really hate me or something."

"You can never be certain if someone hates you until they send you a bomb in the mail," Jamil joked. "As your body is blown to smithereens, then you can be certain that you're not liked."

Nat spotted a piece of black cloth sticking out from under the tree trunk. She reached down and pulled hard. The cloth tore and Nat flew backward, landing on her butt.

"Nice move!" Wall observed. "I give you a six-point-five."

"Very funny," Nat replied as she examined the black cloth. "It's a bandanna."

"So?" Jamil shrugged. "Let's move this tree so we can ride."

Nat stuck the bandanna in her pocket. Together they pushed. The tree didn't budge.

"I bet the person who cut down the pine left this bandanna," she grunted.

"Whew!" Wall said as he leaned against the tree. "Give me that." He snagged the bandanna hanging out of Nat's pocket and wiped his brow. "You know Ian Atkins wears a bandanna just like this. Mrs. Kirby always makes him take it off in class."

"Rea—" Nat began to answer, but her attention was quickly diverted when she noticed the odd look on Wall's face.

Silently, he pointed to a shadow lurking behind a tree about fifty feet away. Someone was watching them!

The shadow froze. Then it disappeared behind a tree.

"Bear!" Jamil yelled.

"No, doofus!" Nat shouted as she broke into a run. "Human!"

Wall, Kevin, and Jamil fell in behind Nat as she crashed through the woods.

"Hey," Nat called out. "Stop!"

Ahead, the shadow moved into an opening in the forest canopy. A splash of light washed over its back, and the crew was able to make out a gray hooded sweatshirt with the letters HVCC—the initials for Hoke Valley Community College—on the back.

Then the person disappeared behind a huge rock. When Nat reached it, the shadow was nowhere in sight.

"Lost him!" Nat cried.

"Look!" Jamil choked, out of breath, as he reached Nat. He was pointing to a clearing hidden by the rock.

Nat, Wall, and Kevin followed him about a hundred feet to the clearing. "Check this out!"

"Wow!" Nat replied as she came up behind Jamil into the clearing. "I never knew this was here."

"What a find!" Wall said. He ran across the clearing and onto a ramp that came off the side of a hill. "Cool ramps!" He leaped off and faked a 360 tail whip.

Nat knelt in the dirt and pointed to a tire track. "BMXers."

"This must be where the thrashers come after school," Wall said admiringly. "I always see them take off together and wondered where they went."

"This rocks," Jamil added. "And it makes perfect sense after all the static they got last summer."

The previous year, the Hoke Valley Town Council confined skateboarders, in-line skaters, and BMXers to the school blacktop. The town ordinance stated that any nonmotorized vehicle could be used to get from one place to another in the town center, but could not be used for tricks, except in the designated locations. Some kids had been lobbying for a skate park to be built, but there hadn't been much enthusiasm from adults in town.

"Maybe they're the ones who cut down the tree," Nat suggested. "That makes a lot more sense than Phil. I was silly to think it was him. He's put too much work into the Bear Claw over the years to let it fail."

"Maybe you're right," Kevin said. "But it probably didn't have to do with ruining the Bear Claw."

"You think they were just protecting their place?" Wall asked.

Mirra's Spinning!

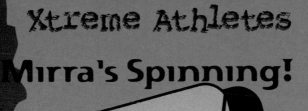

Bicycle stuntman Dave Mirra

Dave Mirra has been riding since he was a kid in upstate New York. He and his brother, Tim, lived on a street where everyone had a bike and everyone rode. Dave became fascinated simply with doing stunts. He never stopped, and he turned his passion into a job. He's been competing since 1987, and has consistently taken first place in both street and halfpipe competitions—including ESPN X Games events—which has earned him the reputation of being one of the top riders in the country.

Dave lives in Greenville, North Carolina, but has plans to move to Raleigh, and eventually open a skate park.

No footed Can-Can
on vertical halfpipe

No handed air
on a vertical halfpipe

Back flip fakie
on a vertical halfpipe

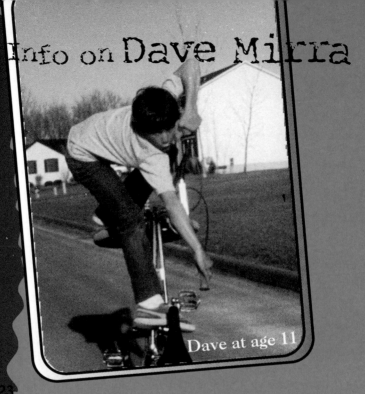

Dave at age 11

Age: 23

Most memorable competition: The 1997 X Games competition, because I rode my best and pulled off perfectly all the tricks I had planned.

Favorite athlete: Michael Jordan, because of his professionalism; he always puts in 100 percent.

Favorite stunt bike: The Haro Dave Mirra Signature Series.

What I like best about my sport: Expressing myself; actions speak louder than words!

Favorite thing to do on a Saturday: Ride all day with friends is number one, but washing my car or playing golf is cool.

Favorite pig-out foods: Pizza, subs, ice cream, bagels with lots of cream cheese!

Favorite movie: *Shawshank Redemption*.

"That makes sense," Jamil said. "Ian told me at school the other day that he feels like a criminal with this new ordinance."

"Ian," Nat said. "He's a BMXer and he always wears a bandanna. He's definitely a possible suspect." Suddenly, she spotted the entrance to an old, boarded-up mine hidden in the rocky hill. She kicked the boards and one of them bounced loose. "Hey," Nat whispered. She pointed to the loose board.

As the other three came over to check out the mine, Nat put her finger to her lips. "Shhhh. The mystery person could be hiding in here."

Wall slid the board sideways and started to go in, but Nat grabbed him by the shirttail and darted in before him. She crouched and crawled through the opening.

"Agggghhh!" Nat let out an earsplitting scream.

Nat quickly scrambled back out on her hands and knees right through Wall's legs. "I'm out of here!"

"What happened?" Jamil asked.

Nat made a disgusted face and held up her hand. It was smeared with thick, light-brown goop. "Get me a water bottle!"

"What is it?" Kevin asked.

"What do you think it is?" Nat said. "Maybe you'd like to lick it. Have a snack."

"I think I'm going to get sick," Kevin said as he backed away.

Nat started to wipe it off on one of the boards nailed to the mine's entrance, but Wall grabbed her hand and brought it to his face.

"Gross!" Jamil gasped. "She was only kidding."

Wall sniffed.

"What?" Nat asked.

"Peanut butter," Wall said. "It's from someone's sand-wich."

Nat stuck her hand out at Kevin. "Lunch?" she laughed and grabbed a fistful of leaves and wiped herself off. "Now I'm going to smell like peanut butter for the rest of the day." She cleaned her hand as best she could. "And I hate peanut butter!" she moaned.

"That's a whole lot better than what you might have smelled like," Kevin said pinching his nose.

Jamil ducked into the mine and found the remains of a pb&j sandwich. He kicked it out with his sneaker.

"Who brought a pb&j up here?" Wall asked. He poked the sandwich with a stick. "It's fresh. The bread isn't stale."

Nat stuck her head back into the mine shaft. "You think someone's living in here?"

"Naw," Kevin answered. "The dirt bikers are probably hanging in there, using it for a crib."

Jamil and Wall checked out a pile of lumber at the edge.

"Hey!" Kevin called. "Look at this!" He held up a large flashlight and a pickax.

Nat ran over and grabbed the flashlight out of Kevin's hand. "Let's explore!"

"I'll wait out here," Wall said. "And make sure the mine doesn't cave in."

"That's positive thinking," Kevin said as he slapped Wall on the back.

Nat led Kevin and Jamil into the mine on their hands

and knees. About ten feet inside, the mine shaft opened up wide enough to stand.

"This is creepy," Nat whispered.

Kevin let out an eerie, deep laugh.

"Shhh!" Nat cut him off. "What if that person is still in here?"

The mine was reinforced with thick timber, and looked secure. The air was stale and heavy with dust. Nat inched forward, keeping the flashlight trained on the tunnel ahead. Jamil and Kevin followed Nat closely behind. Nat ran the light along the side of the tunnel, and Jamil spotted something glittering. He quickly reached around Nat and grabbed the flashlight pointing it back at the wall.

"Gold!" Jamil gasped.

"Look!" Kevin said as he ran his hand along the edge of the vein of gold. "Tool marks."

"Somebody's been mining this," Nat said.

"This is a monster amount of gold," Jamil added. He hit the vein with the edge of the flashlight hoping to knock a piece off.

"Let's get the pick," Nat suggested.

Kevin ran and got it. When he came back inside, he handed the pick to Nat. She took a big swing at the vein and lopped off a good-size chunk of gold.

As they climbed out of the mine, Nat held up the gold nugget to Wall.

"This mystery has just gotten *really* interesting!" Wall shouted. He took the gold from Nat and looked at it more closely. "This'll pay for new bikes for everybody!"

"Rockin'!" Jamil exclaimed. "I'm going dual suspension all the way."

"Wait a minute," Nat said. "Well, now we know

another possible reason someone is trying to keep us off this trail. This gold is being mined by someone who doesn't want us to know about it," Nat explained. "That's why the trail has been blocked off. Otherwise, don't you think you would have heard about this gold mine? There hasn't been gold mined in these mountains for a hundred years." Hoke Valley was originally a mining town. After Central City, it was the richest area for precious metals in Colorado.

"So who do you think it is?" Kevin speculated. "Ian and his BMX dudes? All of our clues point to them so far."

"Or Phil," Nat added. "Maybe this is the real reason he wants the Bear Claw to take a different course. This could be his *real* high school project—becoming a millionaire."

"It could be anyone," Kevin continued. "Gold means grown-ups would be interested."

"Othello Mack lives right over this ridge," Jamil added. "Mr. Stevens is out of work and he lives just down the other way. I mean, we don't really have clear evidence of who it is."

"Who cares?" Wall said. "What I care about is what I'm spending my cut on."

"A brand-new mountain bike with clipless pedals and full suspension," Nat said. "Then a new snowboard and a new computer and . . ."

"A motorcycle!" Kevin interrupted.

"And fill the woods with the smell of gas and noise pollution," Nat countered. "Anyway, we better get back and move that tree before somebody else complains about it."

"But it's too heavy for us to move," Wall said.

"We're going to have to cut it up with a saw," Kevin said. "But where are we going to find a saw?"

"My dad has a chain saw," Wall told them. "We heat our cabin with cord wood. I've been splitting logs since I can remember."

"Could you get it?" Kevin asked excitedly.

Wall grabbed his bike. "I'll go check with my dad."

"Wait!" Jamil called after Wall. "I've got a quicker solution. Charlie Stevens is a friend of my dad's. I bet he'll lend us some tools to move this trunk."

"Cool!" Nat said. "Let's go." She grabbed her bike.

"Lead the way," Wall said to Jamil.

Jamil took them through a cut in the woods where Mountain Electric ran its poles. They had to carry their bikes most of the way and bushwhack through some low brush.

"So who is this guy Stevens?" Wall asked. He'd only been living in Hoke Valley for a month so he didn't know many people.

"Charlie Stevens got laid off at the sawmill when it closed last year," Jamil explained. "He's been doing odd jobs like cutting cord wood and doing carpentry work ever since. My dad hired him to remodel the men's locker room in the lodge last fall and they became friends. From what I understand, he's just getting by."

"But will he lend us a saw?" Nat asked.

"I hope so," Jamil said. "He's a pretty nice guy."

Nat suddenly stopped dead in her tracks. "Wait!" she called. "I just put it together. He's cutting down trees?"

"Yeah," Jamil replied.

"And a tree has been cut down . . . ," Nat continued.

"No, no," Jamil said waving his hands. "It couldn't be him. He's too nice, and besides he wouldn't cut just one tree and leave it."

"Okay," Nat said skeptically, "if you say so. But let's not let him off the suspect list that easy."

As they came over the crest, Jamil spotted the long drive into the Stevenses' camp. They all climbed on their bikes and rode in.

The echo of a basketball bouncing on hard packed dirt reached them long before they saw who was playing.

Tyler and Tara Stevens, Charlie Stevens's sixteen-year-old twins, were playing one-on-one in the driveway. It looked like Tara was getting the best of Tyler. She drained one three-pointer after another.

"Another from downtown!" she shouted as she swished the third one in a row.

Tyler rebounded and bounced the ball to Tara to take out again. Then he rushed her and banged his shoulder into her elbow as she jumped to shoot.

"Foul!" Nat yelled. She put her fingers in her mouth and whistled loudly.

Nat and the gang knew Tyler and Tara from around Hoke Valley. Tyler was an awesome BMXer and tight with Ian, while Tara was a big skier and star of the women's high school basketball team.

"Hey!" Tara waved. "You guys are out early for a Sunday."

"No kidding," Jamil said giving Nat a sideways glance that she ignored.

"You guys are up early, too," Nat said.

Tara laughed. "Mom won't let us sleep past seven. She says it's bad for the spirit, but I think she's worried we won't have time to get all our chores done if we don't get up early."

"What brings you here?" Tyler cut in. "Are you lost?"

Taken aback by Tyler's abruptness, Nat hesitated before she replied. "Uh . . . well, we're working on the course for the Bear Claw . . ."

"And somebody cut down a tree across the trail," Jamil added. "And we were wondering if we could borrow a saw from your dad."

"Yeah, right," Ty smirked.

Nat glanced over at Kevin as if to say, What's his problem?

"Cool," Tara said. "You're working on the race. You going to compete?"

Nat nodded.

"That sounds like fun," Tara said. "Well, I'll talk to my dad about lending you a saw, but I really don't think he'll do it. He's pretty protective about his tools. He won't even let us use them."

"I feel my ears burning," a voice called from inside the house. "Is someone talking about me?" Just then, Mr.

Stevens appeared on the steps to the house.

When he spotted Jamil in the driveway, his face lit up. "Well, well, well! How's your father? I haven't seen him in a month of Sundays."

"He's doing great, but he's got a million things to do that he was putting off while the season was going strong," Jamil explained. "We're here to see if we could borrow a saw." Jamil told Mr. Stevens about the pine tree blocking the Bear Claw's course.

"Don't worry about it," Mr. Stevens said as he waved his hand. "I'll do it myself. Consider it taken care of."

"Thanks, Mr. Stevens! You're a lifesaver," Nat replied.

"I'll see if I can get over there this afternoon," Mr. Stevens promised.

The gang hopped on their bikes and rode back toward the singletrack at the other end of the trail and the Bear Claw's final sprint along Mack Road. They went back down the cut in the woods and pedaled down the thin ribbon of trail that was the last half kilometer before the sprint.

Jamil zoomed ahead of everyone. Standing off his seat to absorb the bumps with his legs, he came around what seemed like an easy turn, but he suddenly had to slam on his brakes.

"Stop!" he shouted to the others behind him. Then he spun his rear tire around and slid sideways down on his bike, just slipping below a taut strand of barbed wire.

"Wipe out!" Wall yelled as he crashed into Jamil and fell on top of him. "What, did you forget how to ride a bike?" Their bodies and bikes twisted in a tangled mess.

"Barbed wire does that to you," Jamil remarked as he pushed Wall's foot out of his face.

Jamil snapped the strand of barbed wire above him.

Wall rolled off Jamil and stood. "Mountain bike limbo is not part of the race."

Nat laid her bike on the ground and ripped off a handwritten sign hanging from the wire. NO TRESPASSING.

"Look at this," Nat said. She waved the sign at her friends. "Now both ends of the singletrack are blocked."

"Someone doesn't want us on this trail," Kevin said.

Nat snorted. "But this is public land."

Suddenly, heavy footsteps crashed through the woods. A massive figure, moving stiffly like the Frankenstein monster, plowed through the brush and

of a baseball cap. The figure growled like a mountain lion.

"Get off my land!" the shadow shouted as he stepped into the light.

"Mr. Mack!" Jamil gasped.

Othello Mack was a hulking, old contractor, who in retirement had become an amateur archaeologist and historian. He was very active in the Hoke Valley Historical Society, but that wasn't what the kids thought of when they saw him. His most distinguishing characteristic was the longest nose hairs in existence. They looked like some kind of strange antennae.

"You're Ned Smith's kid, aren't you?" Mr. Mack said accusingly. His nose antennae quivered as he spoke.

Jamil nodded, too afraid to speak.

"Well, you kids are trespassing on my land," Mr. Mack declared.

"We're sorry," Nat apologized. "We didn't know." She was horrified at the thought that there might be one more problem with the course. She held up the No Trespassing sign and asked, "Is this yours?"

"Huh?" Mr. Mack seemed surprised. "No, but it should be. I should have thought of that myself. It's a darn good idea, because most of this land is private property."

"Private property?" Nat repeated. "I could have sworn it was public land. That's what Mr. Clary said."

"Nick Clary?" Mr. Mack asked.

Nat nodded. "He's president of the Bear Claw and

said it was okay for the course to go through here," she said nervously.

"Not on my land it won't," Mack growled. "This land belongs to me and Charlie Stevens. Nobody has a right to ride here, not racers and not any other bikers. You're tearing up the woods!" He ripped his cap off his head and slapped it against his leg.

The kids flinched.

Mr. Mack marched back through the woods in the direction of his farm.

"Uh, I think we've got a problem," Kevin muttered.

"No kidding," Nat said.

"Yeah," Jamil piped up. "Those have got to be the nastiest nose antennae in existence."

"The only nose antennae in existence," Wall cracked.

They carefully cleared the trail of the barbed wire, making sure they didn't get caught on it. Nat folded the sign and put it in her pocket.

"Let's get out of here before he comes back," Wall suggested. "But I think we better check property lines at Town Hall."

Nat looked at Wall with surprise. "You can do that?" Wall seemed to know a lot of strange but useful things. "Cool. We'll check it out later," Nat said.

They took Mack Road back to town. None of them was in the mood to race the last part of the course. Instead, they tried to work out a plan about what to do about Mr. Mack.

"Do you think he's right?" Jamil asked.

"Can't be," Nat insisted as she wove her bike between Wall and Kevin. "That land is public."

"I think he'd know what land he owns," Kevin said.

Nat sighed. "I'll tell Mr. Clary about it after school tomorrow. And then we'll look it up at Town Hall. He'll be thrilled that another problem has come up. Maybe I shouldn't run the show. I seem to be jinxed."

"Do you think Mr. Mack's the one who's mining the gold?" Wall asked. He was cruising no-handed behind the others now.

Kevin glanced back at him. "Makes sense. He's certainly the person who would know about it since he's an expert on local history."

"Don't tell Mr. Clary about the gold," Jamil suggested. "Let's keep it our secret for now."

"Yeah," Wall added. "I want my cut. If we tell Mr. Clary, we might have to turn it over to some adult."

"All right. I'll keep quiet about the gold at least until we find out who owns the gold mine," Nat agreed. "I could use some spare change." She paused. "Like enough for college and a yacht. Maybe we can even use some of the gold for conservation projects and mountain biking."

"Yes!" Jamil shouted in triumph.

"I'm going to buy myself a satellite dish," Wall said dreamily.

*   *   *

Monday afternoon at school, Kevin slammed his locker shut and turned to Nat. "I'm going to be a millionaire by my birthday on Saturday."

Together they headed down the hall to Mr. Clary's science class.

"I'm going to set up a state-of-the-art lab to test snowboards," Kevin said.

Nat rolled her eyes.

"Oh, I almost forgot," Kevin said as he stood in the middle of the hall spreading his arms dramatically. "I'm going to carve every deep powder spot on the globe— from the Andes to the Himalayas."

"Hurry, Richie Rich," Nat said. "I want to catch Mr. Clary before he leaves." She headed straight for Mr. Clary's classroom.

When she got to the door, Nat grabbed the door-knob, but suddenly froze when she heard voices on the other side of the door.

"I really don't think Nat is up to the challenge," one voice insisted. "She's too young and, to speak truthfully, I don't think a girl can do this job."

Nat slowly and quietly cracked open the door.

Inside, Phil Speck was speaking to Mr. Clary. "I think I should take over the Bear Claw."

Nat's face turned beet red. She threw her shoulder into the door and slammed it wide open. "I can too do it!" Nat said firmly as she marched into the room.

"Oh, no," Phil said.

Nat gulped, trying to stifle tears. "Why can't you help me instead of trying to make me fail?"

Phil shook his head. "You're not doing the job."

"I am, too," Nat protested. "It's just that someone is trying to sabotage the trail." Nat breathed deeply to calm herself. She knew it wouldn't be good to start a fight in front of Mr. Clary, but she couldn't hold back completely. "By the way you're acting, I wouldn't be surprised if you're behind it all."

With all the recent evidence, Nat had been pretty convinced she could rule Phil out as a suspect. Now, she wasn't so sure.

"What?" Phil said, surprised.

"Hold it right there," Mr. Clary said. "Let's not start accusing each other."

"I've got to go," Phil said as he turned to leave. "I just hope you can handle it, Nat, especially now that the course is going to be changed."

Nat started to open her mouth, but Mr. Clary held up his hand to stop her.

He turned to Nat. "We have to talk."

Nat and Kevin slipped into the desks in the front row.

After the door to the classroom closed, Mr. Clary leaned against his desk and crossed his arms. "Don't worry. I'm not moving the race."

Nat relaxed a bit. Maybe she wasn't going to be fired.

"We've already printed the maps. It's too late to change." Mr. Clary paused. "Though I seriously considered it after hearing from Phil what bad shape the course is in."

Nat gulped. Kevin looked down at his hands folded on the desktop.

"Besides," he said as he looked Nat in the eye. "The pine tree has been moved so there aren't any more obstacles on the trail, right?"

Nat swallowed hard. "Uh, not really." She hesitated, afraid to tell Mr. Clary the latest disaster.

"Spill it," Mr. Clary prodded.

Nat took a deep breath. "Okay, this is the story." She paused to bolster her courage. "Yesterday, we ran into Othello Mack who said that the trail cut across his land."

"You've got to be kidding." Mr. Clary slapped his

forehead. "I could have sworn that trail was on public land. I checked out the maps at the ranger station."

"So we're fine," Nat said with relief.

"Well," Mr. Clary hesitated. "I'm not so sure. The maps were pretty confusing. Part of the course does go over the Stevenses' property, but Charlie doesn't mind riders there."

Mr. Clary pulled out his map and laid it on his desk. Nat and Kevin gathered around it. He circled the section of singletrack where they had been having trouble.

"See this part." He was pointing to the spot where the pine was cut down. "This is on the Stevenses' property." Now, he pointed to a spot a little below that. "This, however, could cross Mack's land, but only for a hundred feet at the most."

"How could he complain about that?" Nat asked.

"I don't know, but we should check the property lines at Town Hall to make sure we're not mistaken," Mr. Clary replied.

Nat flushed. She wished now that she'd gone to Town Hall this morning, so that she could show Mr. Clary how responsible and on top of things she was. "I'm definitely planning on checking out the maps," Nat assured him.

A look of relief washed over Mr. Clary's face. "Thanks. I'm swamped with the fifty million things I've got to do before the race on Saturday."

"We're on our way," Nat said as she and Kevin dashed out of the classroom.

Outside, the clock over the Hoke Valley Town Hall rang.

"We're sunk," Kevin said.

"What do you mean?" Nat asked.

"They're closed," Kevin explained. "Town Hall closes at four. The clock just rang four times."

"First thing after school tomorrow!" Nat said.

"No problem," Kevin replied.

"I just hope that trail doesn't run through Mack's property," Nat wished.

"I know," Kevin seconded. "There's no way he'll let us ride."

"We don't have time to waste," Nat called to her friends as she bounded out of school Tuesday afternoon.

"Town Hall doesn't close for an hour," Kevin said. "Relax."

"Not until I know who owns that trail," Nat said. "It's already Tuesday. There's only four days until the race. If we've got to change the course or fight Mack, we have to do it yesterday."

The four of them marched down the street to Town Hall.

The small park in front of the building was a favorite spot for kids to hang out. This afternoon the sparse grass was packed with kids playing Frisbee, sitting on the benches, or lying on the ground.

Sitting a little ways to the left of the front steps was Tyler Stevens. His electric blue BMX bike with chrome pegs was lying at his feet; right next to it was a brand-new all-black BMX bike with a custom Jax Max frame.

As the crew walked up the sidewalk, Ty reached into his pocket and pulled out a package of peanut butter crackers. He ripped open the wrapper and shoved a couple in his mouth. He was watching a bunch of kids playing Ultimate Frisbee and didn't notice Nat and her friends.

Just then, Ian Atkins darted through the front door of the Town Hall building. Nat and the others watched as he waved to Ty and flashed a triumphant thumbs-up. "What's that all about?" Kevin asked as he watched Ian hook up with Ty at the bottom of the steps.

"They must be up to something," Wall muttered.

"Look," Nat sputtered, "he's wearing a bandanna." She pointed out the red bandanna tied around Ian's head.

"Did you notice what Ty was eating?" Jamil added.

"Peanut butter crackers," Kevin pointed out. "So what? I eat them all the time."

"Remember the pb&j at the mine?" Jamil reminded him.

Nat grinned. "Yeah, and if I remember correctly, you had pb&j for lunch today. I can still remember the awful smell."

"No clue, Sherlock!" Kevin laughed.

"Wait," Nat said. "Why don't we ask Ian a few questions about the thrashers in the woods?" She and her friends headed across the grass toward Ty and Ian.

"What up?" Ian flashed the crew a smile.

"Same old, same old," Nat replied. "But I . . ."

Wall whispered in Nat's ear. "Nothing about the gold."

Ian and Ty gave them an odd look.

Nat nodded. "Oh, Wall was just saying that we saw ramps and BMX tracks by the old mine."

"Yeah, that place rocks," Ian said guardedly. "We've been setting it up to do tricks there." Ian popped a wheelie on his brand-new bike and stood on his rear pegs for a couple of seconds. Then, he spun a 360, but it wasn't perfect. "Oops!" he said as he caught himself from falling.

"Heavy stuff!" Wall said admiring Ian's trick.

"I like street stunts," Ian explained. "But I'm really glad we found that place. It's perfect for dirt riding." He stood on his front wheel and spun his bike around. Ty copied Ian's move.

"It must have been tough to get to, with that pine tree blocking the trail," Nat said.

"It wasn't really in our way," Ian replied.

"Maybe not in your way," Kevin said, "but it looks like someone's trying to keep mountain bikers away from the clearing."

"Thrashers don't care if mountain bikers ride trails," Ian countered. "In fact, anybody is welcome. The place is open." Ian hopped on his bike.

"Well, someone cut down that tree on purpose." Nat pulled the black bandanna from her back pocket and waved it in the air. "And it was someone who wears a bandanna like this one. We found it by the tree."

Ian stood with his bike between his legs and raised his hands palm out in an exaggerated gesture of inno-

his hands palm out in an exaggerated gesture of inno-cence. But Ty froze, his eyes fixed in a strange stare on the black cloth.

"Duh! Not thrashers, man." Ian pointed to his friends across the park. They were wearing the same type of red bandanna he was. "We all wear red ones."

"What are you doing at Town Hall then if you're not interested in the mine?" Kevin asked.

Wall kicked him lightly on the leg. "I told you, don't say anything about the gold," he hissed.

"Mine? Whatever. I'm only here 'cause my mom works here," he muttered. "I have to tell her where I'm going after school."

As Ian and Ty left, Wall asked, "Do you really think Ian is behind the tree and the barbed wire?"

"I don't know," Nat replied. "But did you see the way Ty looked at the bandanna? He looked so guilty. I'm real-ly curious about how they got those bikes. They looked brand-new."

"Ian's a custom job," Wall remarked. "That means major cash."

"Major gold," Kevin cracked. "I bet they sold some of the gold from the mine."

"A definite possibility," Nat agreed.

"And don't forget the peanut butter crackers. Ty was eating them just now," Jamil reminded them.

"Yeah, peanut butter is the clue that's going to break open the case," Wall cracked.

Jamil stuck his hands in his pockets and mumbled,

"Well, whatever."

"So, like, look what time it is." Kevin stared up at the clock on top of the building. It read three forty-five.

"Let's move it," Nat urged. The crew made a beeline for the town clerk's office inside the building.

In the town clerk's office, a young, ponytailed guy was leaning over a desk, talking on a phone and making notes. The gang walked up to the counter and waited. When the ponytailed guy hung up, he looked over at Nat and her friends and raised his eyebrows.

"Hi, we need to look at the town map," Nat said in a businesslike tone.

"Sure," the guy said, and grabbed a huge binder off a row of file cabinets. He dropped it on the counter and went back to his desk.

Nat opened the binder. The town was divided into sectors. Each sector was numbered and mapped in this book. Nat flipped through the pages and stopped at sector fourteen.

"This isn't it," Kevin said as he leaned over Nat's shoulder.

"No, this is where the race begins, right near the resort lodge," Nat explained. She placed her finger about three inches from a square that indicated the lodge. "See, the trail goes off this way through the resort's property." Nat ran her finger along a dotted line that showed the trail.

When she reached the edge of the page she turned to the next. "Then, the course comes up along this ridge and follows these switchbacks until the singletrack that leads to the edge of the resort's property."

Nat turned the page again. She examined the map. "Hmmmm. I can't quite make out where the trail leads," she muttered.

"It's not marked," Kevin said.

"Do you think it goes this way?" Wall asked as he pointed to the center of a wash between two low ridges.

"Well, if you're right," Nat replied, "then that means Mr. Stevens owns the land Mr. Mack blocked off with the barbed wire. But on the other hand, if the trail goes along this side of the wash, then it's in Mr. Mack's property." Nat shook her head in confusion.

"But if it runs on the other side of the wash, it's on public land," Wall said. "The Stevenses sure have a weird piece of property. It runs like a finger down the middle of the wash between Mr. Mack's property and public land."

"Well, I can say that the mine is definitely owned by Mr. Mack," Kevin said. "Even if we can't tell where the trail runs."

"Excuse me," Nat called to the clerk.

The clerk came over from his desk and looked at the map. "What's up?"

"Well, we're having trouble figuring out property lines," Nat explained.

The clerk leaned over the map.

"See here," Nat said as she pointed to the section they were confused about. "We can't figure out where the trail runs. Does it run through the Mack property, the

Stevenses', or public land?"

The clerk shrugged. "Beats me. You better check with Leah Anderson. She's been here forever. She can tell you about every inch of this town."

"Is she here?" Nat asked.

"Sorry, she'll be in tomorrow," the clerk answered. "Are you done with this?"

"Tomorrow," Nat grumbled. "But we need to know now!"

"There's nothing I can do," the clerk replied apologetically. "I wish I knew more, because you're not the only one interested in where the property lines are in this wash. Someone else asked to see this map earlier today."

"Was it a kid wearing a red bandanna?" Nat asked. She remembered Ian flashing the thumbs-up sign as he left Town Hall. Maybe he'd been intentionally acting confused when Wall mentioned the mine.

The clerk shook his head. "Nope. It was some old guy with . . . well . . . he was old."

Nat glanced at Kevin. "What did he look like?" Nat asked the clerk.

"About my height, I guess," the clerk said. "Gray hair. Flannel shirt." He paused. "The man looked like he might have needed a shave."

"Might have?" Jamil cut in.

"Well," the clerk said, "not exactly a shave."

"A haircut," Jamil persisted.

"No, not really a haircut," the clerk replied. "But a trim." He waved his hand under his nose.

A smile spread across Jamil's face. "Othello Mack."

"The guy had a humongous nest of hair coming out of his nose?" Wall blurted.

The clerk just nodded.

"Uh, thanks," Nat said as they left. Outside, they sat on a bench in the park in front of the building.

"None of this makes sense," Nat groaned to her friends. "I could have sworn it was Phil who did this, and then I was convinced Ty and Ian were behind it all ten minutes ago. Now Othello Mack . . ."

"Let's look at it logically," Kevin said. "Suspect one," Kevin held up his thumb. "Phil Speck doesn't want you to be in charge. He thinks the course is all wrong. Two." He held up his index finger. "Ian, Ty, and the BMXers have found a great dirt track just off the trail. They're having trouble finding places to ride without static. Three." He added his middle finger to his other two. "Mr. Mack doesn't want anyone riding on the trail, possibly because of the gold mine."

"They've all got good motives," Wall said.

"The important thing is to get the gold before the culprit does!" Jamil insisted. "And of course to follow up on the peanut butter clue."

"Well, in any case, you'd better call Mr. Clary and tell him there's a good chance that the course may run over Mr. Mack's property," Kevin suggested to Nat.

"Good idea," Nat said as she dug a quarter out of her pocket. She headed across the street to the pay phone in front of the Quik Market. Her friends followed, but they went into the market for snacks.

"Get me something, too," Nat called to them.

"Peanut butter crackers?" Jamil smiled.

"NOT!" Nat answered "I'll see you guys tomorrow." She laughed.

Nat slipped the quarter into the slot. She dialed Mr. Clary's home phone number. She was worried that Mr. Clary would think she'd failed in her job, and would replace her, but he was pretty calm and good-natured about it.

At the end of Nat's explanation, he suggested, "Why don't we meet with Othello tomorrow after school and talk to him about the race? Maybe if we talk to him together, he won't be so against it."

Nat flushed at the thought of Mr. Clary having to step in and help her. She really hoped she'd be able to do this all herself, but after her last encounter with Mr. Mack she knew she wasn't going to get anywhere on her own. "Okay."

"We can explain that mountain biking doesn't hurt the forest," Mr. Clary added. "I'll give him a call and set up a meeting."

"Thanks, Mr. Clary." Nat hung up.

As she turned onto the marketplace, she spotted a poster for the Bear Claw on Saturday. Her spirits sank at the sight of it. Everything seemed to be going wrong. The race might have to be canceled or moved if she couldn't straighten out the course problems. And it would be her fault. Then Phil would be right. She couldn't handle the responsibility. And she didn't even want to think about the gold mine! She couldn't let herself get distracted by thoughts of getting rich quick—although then maybe she could have her own bedroom . . .

She shook off thoughts of a new custom mountain bike and turned her mind to homework. For the first time in her entire life, the thought of doing math homework seemed pleasant. At least she could solve algebra problems!

Long after Nat had done all her math problems and had put the finishing touches on a book report, she was brushing her teeth and getting ready for bed.

Suddenly, the phone rang. It startled Nat. Nobody ever called this late.

Nat spit the toothpaste out of her mouth. "I'll get it!" she shouted.

"No, I'll get it," Ella yelled. She was already in bed, but unfortunately not asleep.

Nat had a head start, however, and picked up the phone just as Ella barreled around the corner into the kitchen.

Nat stuck her tongue out at her younger sister. "Go to bed," she mouthed.

Ella made a face and mimicked Nat. "Go to bed. La de da."

"Nat?" the voice on the line asked.

"Yeah, who's this?" Nat said.

"Tara Stevens," she said. "I'm sorry about calling so

late, but I was hoping to talk to you about what happened to Phil Speck on the trail today."

"Phil? On the trail?" Nat gasped. She sank to the floor. "What happened?"

"You mean you don't know?" Tara sounded surprised.

"No," Nat said. "Tell me."

"There was an accident on the trail where the tree was cut down." Tara paused. "And Phil ended up in the hospital."

"Hospital?" Nat echoed in disbelief.

"It's terrible. From what I hear," Tara explained, sounding as upset as Nat felt, "Phil blew his tire out on some barbed wire strung across the trail and went out of control."

"Was he hurt bad?" Nat asked. She tried to breathe slowly to calm herself.

"His mom says he's okay," Tara reassured Nat, "but I think he broke his leg."

"Oh, no!" Nat groaned.

"It's just horrible that something like that happened. Still, I'm really worried that someone else might get hurt," Tara confided to Nat. "I think it'd be a lot safer if the Bear Claw on Saturday was moved to a new location."

"What?" Nat screamed. This is the last thing she wanted to hear. "You've got to be kidding. We've already printed the maps. There must be some other solution."

"I really think it would be safer if it was moved," Tara persisted.

"Why? What do you know that I don't?" Nat asked.

"Nothing really," Tara said hesitantly.

Nat suspected that she was holding something back. "Come on, Tara," Nat pressed. "I've got to know, especially if I'm going to change the course. Didn't your dad move the tree?"

"Yeah, he did," Tara answered. "But it looks like that's not your only obstacle."

"What am I going to do?" Nat cried. "But maybe that's the end of the trouble on the trail."

"Well, I wouldn't be so sure," Tara explained. "I hate to tell on anyone, but I overheard Ty talking to some BMXers. Anyway, the BMXers said something about mountain bikers being a real pain. They said they didn't want all those bikers in the Bear Claw race ratting out their spot. I'm afraid they might do something even more serious."

Furiously, Nat spun the tires on her mountain bike in a mud puddle as a loud groan seemed to vibrate through her body. As she pedaled faster, the groan seemed to become clearer.

"Move . . . . Moooooove!"

Nat pedaled harder, but she couldn't seem to get through the puddle. Suddenly, she saw a BMX biker come flying off the top of a tree and sail down toward her.

"Agggggghhhh!" she screamed and tried to duck.

The BMXer ignored her and spun a 360 on his front tire right next to Nat, splashing her with black mud.

Somehow she finally broke free of the mud, just as the massive tree that the biker came out of was about to crush her.

"Help!" she screamed and pumped her legs harder. But now her bike moved as if it was riding through molasses. The faster she pedaled, the slower she went.

She checked to see if she was in granny gear and she wasn't. She couldn't understand what was making her go so slow.

Then, she felt a tap on her shoulder. She turned around and saw Phil Speck holding onto her bike frame.

He broke into the eeriest laugh she had ever heard. She squirmed to jump off her bike when the laugh somehow turned into a scream. Her scream. As she fell . . . and fell . . . and . . .

Thud!

Nat jolted awake as she hit the floor. She had fallen out of bed. She realized it was just a dream and sighed in relief.

Her alarm clock buzzed. She reached up and turned it off.

"I hope I never dream like that," Ella whispered from her bed across the room. She was sitting up with her arms wrapped around her legs.

Nat gulped and yawned. "It's no fun." She stood up and stretched. "I feel exhausted," she said, scratching her head on the way to the bathroom. As she got cleaned up, she tried to shake off the anxious feeling she was having after last night's call from Tara. She hurried to get dressed. She needed to talk to her friends about Tara's warning, and it had been too late last night to call them.

Nat waited for her friends at the sculpture in front of the school. It was some sort of modern sculpture of curved bronze and stone that was supposed to be Mount Olley. Only it didn't really look like a mountain, just big, rounded shapes that were a target for birds.

Jamil, Kevin, and Wall came up the steps together.

"What's up?" Jamil said.

"Bad news," Nat answered. "And more bad news." She told them about Phil getting hurt and Tara warning them about BMXers.

"It's the curse of the Bear Claw," Wall said eerily. "Every year Nat is destined to organize the Bear Claw Mountain Bike Race at Hoke Valley and every year unexplained phenomena conspire to thwart her efforts."

"Get real," Nat replied. "Somebody's behind this. Since Phil was hurt on the trail he couldn't be the one who sabotaged it. That eliminates one suspect. My bets are on Ian. He's admitted to hanging there."

"Or Tyler," Kevin piped up. "I still think he's been acting suspicious. We should talk to him alone."

"Oh, I almost forgot," Nat remembered. "We also have a meeting with Othello Mack this afternoon."

"Do you think we should split up?" Kevin asked. "Today is Wednesday. Three days to go until the race."

"Right," Nat agreed. "Jamil and Kevin can check out Tyler, while Wall and I go with Mr. Clary. We can meet up afterward at the clearing in the woods and compare notes. Then, we can check out Ian if these leads dead end."

The first bell sounded, and the crew dashed into the building.

*   *   *

After school, Jamil and Kevin hopped on their bikes and

headed straight for the Stevenses' home.

Jamil knocked on the front door, and he and Kevin waited.

No answer.

"Try this," Kevin said as he pushed the doorbell.

"Coming," a voice from inside called.

A minute passed and the front door swung open. Tara stood in front of them. "Oh, hi!" She seemed a little surprised to see them.

Jamil and Kevin put on their friendliest faces.

"Is Tyler around?" Kevin asked.

Tara shook her head. "He's off some place. I never know where."

Jamil and Kevin took this in and tried to think of something else to ask, but couldn't.

"He's riding his bike," Tara volunteered. She started to close the door, but then hesitated. "You know, I'm still worried about that trail. Are you sure it's okay?"

Jamil shrugged. "I don't know, but we've got three days to make it okay."

"I just hope no other bikers get hurt," Tara confided. "Don't you think you should move the course?"

"We might have to," Jamil admitted with an edge of frustration. He dug his hands into his pockets. He glanced up at Tara and noticed the coat rack beside the door. On it hung a gray hooded HVCC sweatshirt. Something in Jamil's brain clicked. He'd seen that sweatshirt before.

"That's a nice sweatshirt," Jamil said as he pointed to it.

Tara turned and glanced over her shoulder. "Yeah, it's pretty nice."

"I always wanted one like that," Jamil continued, "but every time I check out the college bookstore, my size is sold out."

Tara nodded in sympathy. "My mom works at the college. She gave them to Tyler and me for Christmas. If you want, I could ask my mom to keep an eye out for your size."

"Great!" Jamil said.

"Thanks." Kevin waved as they left.

"Later," Tara said. She closed the front door.

In the middle of the driveway Kevin paused. "You know where we've seen that sweatshirt!" he blurted excitedly. "Remember on Saturday when we discovered the tree down?"

"Oh, yeah," Jamil grinned. "Are you thinking what I am?"

"Exactly," Kevin answered. "Tyler!"

"He's got to be the culprit," Jamil said as he smacked his hand with his fist.

Kevin ticked off the reasons. "He lives near the trail so he can get to it whenever he wants. He acted weird when I showed him the black bandanna. He rides BMX bikes, and so has to be wrapped up in making ramps in the clearing. His dad owns a chain saw. And he'd want the gold just as much as anyone, since his dad's out of work."

"And we saw him eating peanut butter!" Jamil reminded Jamil.

reminded Jamil.

Kevin shook his head. "You're a little *stuck* on that clue aren't you?" He laughed.

"Ha, ha," Jamil said. "Hey, while we're here, why don't we scout around for more clues."

"Good idea," Kevin replied. "But what do you think we'll find?"

"Who knows," Jamil said as he headed around the side of the house. He peeked through a window and saw the dining room table covered with chain-saw repair tools.

"Over here," Kevin called. He pointed at the garage. "Maybe we can find some mining tools."

They peered through the small, dirty windows in the garage door.

"That's strange," Jamil said. "Ty's bike is there."

"Then how's he out riding?" Kevin asked.

"He's not," Jamil answered. "But why would Tara lie?"

Jamil and Kevin looked at each other, trying to figure out what this meant.

Othello Mack's house was an old white clapboard farmhouse at the end of Mack Road. Behind the house sat a large barn and silo that were falling apart.

Nat, Wall, and Mr. Clary stepped onto the front porch. The boards under their feet creaked. Mr. Clary knocked once.

Before he could knock again, the door swung open.

"Heard you coming down the road," Mr. Mack explained. "Nobody can sneak up on me out here." He gave a little chuckle. He invited them inside and sat in an overstuffed chair in the front room.

To Nat and Wall's surprise he didn't seem quite as huge and fierce as he did in the woods the other day.

Nat, Wall, and Mr. Clary sat on the edge of the couch.

Mr. Clary cleared his throat. "We just wanted to stop by to explain that mountain bikers aren't going to hurt the woods. In fact, mountain bikers do less damage than hikers because they never leave the trail and trample delicate flora."

Mr. Mack interrupted Mr. Clary. "I'm not worried about the trail. That's not on my property." He looked at Nat and Wall. "It's you kids riding your bikes up there that's damaging an important archaeological site on my property, not to mention the surrounding woods."

"Huh?" Nat replied, dumbfounded.

"You're right," Mr. Clary cut in, "but that's not us. We don't ride bikes off ramps or do anything to change the environment." Mr. Clary launched into a long-winded explanation of mountain biking and ecology.

Nat had heard all this before. Besides, she couldn't look at Mr. Mack's twitching nose hair another second. Her mind began to wander and she glanced around the room. On the coffeetable was a collection of arrowheads. The walls were covered with all kinds of rusted, old tools. Some of them she could make out, others seemed completely foreign. On the wall beside the couch was a bookcase full of dusty, old histories of Colorado and the West.

So he's interested in some old archaeological site, she thought. Then her eyes rested on another book, *Gold Mining in the Old West*. Suddenly, it all came together. At first she hesitated because she wanted to run it by Mr. Clary, but there wasn't time to wait. The Bear Claw was in three days. Nat interrupted Mr. Clary. "So the archaeological site is the gold mine up in the woods?"

Mr. Clary gave Nat a funny look. Then he burst out into a deep, rumbling laugh. "Gold! Is that what you kids think it is?" He shook his head, still laughing. "It's a mine all right, but that's not gold in it."

Nat and Wall looked blankly at him.

"I hate to break it to you," Mr. Mack explained. "But that's pyrite—fool's gold!"

Jamil and Kevin stood in the driveway with their bikes.

"What next?" Jamil asked Kevin.

"I want to know why Tara's lying," Kevin said. "Was she covering for her twin brother? Does she know Ty's involved?" He started for the front door of the Stevenses' house again. Jamil followed.

They rang the doorbell and waited.

No one answered.

Jamil gave Kevin a questioning look. "We know she's home. We just talked to her."

They rang the bell several more times. As they stood there waiting, the door to the garage suddenly slid open.

A figure in a gray, hooded sweatshirt flew out on Ty's electric-blue BMX bike!

"Holy bikes, Batman!" Jamil shouted as he ran to his mountain bike.

"Follow that rider, Robin," Kevin yelled as he began pedaling.

The BMX bike spun out at the edge of the woods.

"Stop!" Jamil yelled.

The rider glanced over his shoulder and was off. His bike crashed through the woods.

Jamil and Kevin were right on the rider's heels.

"Stop!" Jamil yelled.

The rider glanced over his shoulder and was off. His bike crashed through the woods.

Jamil and Kevin were right on the rider's heels.

Jamil surprisingly surged ahead of Kevin, but couldn't gain any ground on the mysterious biker. Even though this biker was riding a BMX bike, he knew how to ride rough terrain. Jamil's and Kevin's twenty-one gears weren't much help in the thick brush. The fact that their bikes rode higher than the BMX bike made it harder to avoid low-hanging limbs.

After Jamil bunny-hopped over a small log on the ground, he pounded his kidneys to a pulp on a washboard. He tried to stand on his bike as he pedaled but the branches held him back. But all that mountain biking practice had helped—he was still on the bike!

When he looked over his shoulder, he saw Kevin sitting in a pile of brush. He biffed into a tangle of branches.

"I'm fine!" he called as he waved Jamil on.

He tucked his head down, grabbed his extension bars, and pumped furiously. The forest floor had leveled out, but the BMX rider was pulling away. The brush was just too thick for Jamil to make better time.

"Ugh!" Jamil bounced into a dip. He came around a big tree and slid into a steep gully. He began to falter, but quickly recovered. When he looked ahead, however, the BMX biker was gone.

Jamil slowed as he came to the clearing where the old

mine was located. He rolled into the grassy glade. It looked like someone had laid a couple of handfuls of hay over this part of the clearing. He figured someone had thrown the hay over a puddle and headed straight through it.

Snap! Jamil did an endo into the grass. He ducked his head and rolled on his shoulder, recovering perfectly from the fall. Someone had hidden barbed wire under the hay!

"Nice move!" Nat shouted as she and Wall came into the clearing from the other side. At the same time Kevin crashed through the brush carrying his bike. "You okay?" he asked as he knelt beside Jamil.

"Sure," Jamil said. He looked over at his bike. "But I've got a flat tire." He stood and released his tire from the front fork.

"What happened?" Wall asked.

Jamil explained how they chased Ty on his BMX bike through the woods and lost him in the clearing.

"Look!" Kevin interrupted Jamil when something metallic flashed from behind a ramp set up in the middle of the clearing. Behind the ramp lay Ty's electric blue bike. "It's got a flat, too," Kevin said as he squeezed the front tire.

"He's got to be in the mine," Wall concluded. "Otherwise, we would have run into him."

"Come on," Nat said. She flicked on her pocket flashlight and slid the loose board to the side. She crawled inside and her friends followed.

Nat slowly washed the beam of light over every inch

Nat gasped.
It wasn't Tyler they'd cornered!

"Tara!" Nat blurted, totally stunned.

Tara tried to smile. "You caught me."

"I thought you were your brother!" Nat blurted.

"So you're really the one who's been blocking the trail!" Kevin exclaimed as they headed for the mine's exit.

In the clearing she began to explain.

"I didn't want anyone to find out about the gold," Tara said.

"The gold!" Kevin cried. He had totally forgotten about it. "So it *was* the mine you were protecting."

"*Forget* about the gold," Wall tried to explain. "Our dreams of endless wealth are over. There is no gold."

"What do you mean forget about it?" Tara cried, almost in tears. "It's what's going to help my dad."

Wall sighed. "No, what I mean is that it's not gold. It's pyrite—fool's gold." He explained what Mr. Mack had told them.

"We're paupers, again," Jamil cried. "Ugh! And I already had my executive jet picked out."

Tara sat in the dirt in total shock. "What a mess. I caused all that trouble for nothing. I'm the one who cut down that tree and strung the barbed wire." Her bottom lip began to tremble. "If I hadn't done that, Phil wouldn't have been hurt." She looked at Nat. "That's why I called you last night. I was hoping to make you change the course so nobody else would get hurt. And I'd still be able to keep people away from the mine."

As they listened, Kevin started to repair the BMX bike with Nat's repair kit.

"Once I realized that you guys thought it was the BMXers who were messing with the course, I tried to encourage your suspicions. I thought it would convince you to change the course."

Nat slapped her forehead. "I never suspected a girl would be behind this."

Jamil laughed. "Don't underestimate them girls," he cracked. "They can build a race course *and* sabotage it. They can do anything."

"Tara, do you know what kind of trouble you caused?" Nat said. "The Bear Claw was almost cancelled because of you. There would have been hundreds of bikers and no race."

"And Phil has a broken leg," Jamil added. "You're lucky he wasn't more seriously hurt."

Tara was crying now. "I know I was wrong, but I did this for my family. Ever since my dad lost his job, things have been really tough. I thought if I could just get us some money. Then I discovered the mine, and I thought all our problems were solved."

"We thought ours were solved, too," Wall muttered.

As Nat watched Tara, her anger began to soften. Even though Tara had almost ruined the race, Nat could understand why she did it. Things could get tough sometimes with her parents' bookstore. Some months she saw them worry over which bills they could pay and which they couldn't. And she always felt helpless. Now she might be able to help someone in a worse bind.

"But wait a minute," Kevin said as he looked up from repairing the flat tires, "how come you threw the blame on the BMXers and didn't mess with them?"

"As you guys have already figured out, I don't plan too well. I didn't think you guys would be so persistent so I thought they could handle the heat. Anyway, my brother's a thrasher," Tara answered. "I figured if I ran into trouble he'd help me out. In the meantime, I planned to just move in and out when they weren't there."

Kevin reinflated the inner tube to check the patch. Then Nat remembered about the black bandanna. She pulled it out of her pocket. "This must be yours."

Tara took the bandanna. "Yeah, where'd you find it?"

"You dropped it by the tree you cut down," Wall explained.

"So all this means that Ty wasn't helping you out?" Nat asked.

Tara shook her head. "I was afraid he'd tell Ian about

the gold—I mean pyrite."

"I still can't believe it's not gold," Kevin moaned as he inserted the tube back in the rim. "That's brutal."

"There goes my Jacuzzi," Jamil muttered longingly.

"I'm really sorry I caused so much trouble," Tara repeated. "Is there anything I can do to make up for it?"

"That's not up to us," Jamil replied. "You've caused a lot of headaches."

Tara hung her head.

"Wait a sec," Wall broke in, "She hasn't broken any laws, has she?"

"Try trespassing and property damage," Kevin said. "This *is* Mr. Mack's land."

"Oh, yeah, I forgot," Wall replied. "But maybe Mr. Mack won't press charges."

"Like I said," Jamil repeated. "It's not up to us."

"But maybe Mr. Clary and Mr. Mack don't have to know," Nat began slowly. "They won't be affected anymore by your sabotage. Phil, on the other hand, you have to make it up to him big time. And you have to make it up to me." Nat paused. "This has been a nightmare!"

"Do I have to tell Phil?" Tara asked in a small voice.

"Definitely," Nat said. "And what he decides to do is up to him. In the meantime, I know just the thing you can do for me."

"What?" Tara said.

"Meet me at Bear Claw on Saturday and I'll tell you then," Nat replied mysteriously.

A worried look crossed Tara's face.

Nat smiled to reassure her. "Don't worry. We're not going to bust you. Everything's pretty much turned out okay . . ."

"Except for Phil," Tara interrupted. "But I'll make it up to him somehow."

"But you better tell your brother not to ride around Mr. Mack's abandoned mine," Wall added. "He's really psycho on people ruining his archaeological site."

Tara crossed her heart. "I promise."

"One last thing." Jamil interrupted with a very serious tone.

Everyone looked at him expectantly.

"Was that your peanut butter sandwich we found in the mine?" Jamil asked.

The gang burst into laughter.

"No, really," Jamil persisted. "We found that sandwich and then we saw Ty eating peanut butter crackers. I'm sure it was a clue."

"Forget the peanut butter, already," Nat cried.

Tara smiled. "You know, Ty and I are exact opposites in a lot of ways, but we definitely have one thing in common. We're both peanut butter fiends. We'd eat peanut butter for every meal of the day if our mom allowed us."

"See!" Jamil said gleefully.

It was a beautiful, dry, sunny day. Perfect for the Bear Claw. Nat was pleased when she arrived early and was able to put the finishing touches on the course without any more disasters.

Mr. Clary met her at the starting line. "I can trust the course is ready?"

"It's perfect!" Nat said with enthusiasm. She and her friends had spent the previous afternoon going over the course on foot to make sure nothing was amiss.

"The tree is gone?" Mr. Clary said.

"Yup!"

"The barbed wire?"

"Yup!"

"The property issue is cleared up?"

"Yup!"

Mr. Clary tossed one end of a banner to Nat and they tied it between two posts. "So who was responsible for all those shennanigans?"

"Well . . . uh . . . It was just a mix-up with some kids," Nat answered evasively. "But it's fixed now."

"Good," Mr. Clary replied and went off to take care of another detail.

About an hour later, everything was ready and Nat sat at the base of a tree and sipped a soda.

"Wow! There must be over a thousand riders here," Jamil exclaimed as he came up to her.

"Hey!" Wall called to them as he elbowed his way through the crowd. "Look at all this cool swag!" He was holding up a pair of Day-Glo orange sunglasses. "They're just throwing them into the crowd by the Huffy Toss."

"The Huffy Toss has already started?" Jamil said.

"Yeah, Kevin tossed a bike fifteen feet and smashed the chain off," Wall explained.

"I want to go next," Jamil yelled.

The gang hurried over to the Huffy Toss. They snaked through the cheering crowd and saw Phil's friend Max take a running start with a bike held above his head. Leaning on crutches, Phil was cheering Max on from the sidelines.

"Arrrgggghhhh!" Max screamed as he heaved the bike as far as he could.

The bike flew about ten feet and bounced another five. But nothing broke off. Kevin was still in the lead.

"Sick!" Jamil yelled. "I got to try this!"

Just then Phil came up beside Nat. "Good luck on the race."

"Thanks," she replied awkwardly. "How's your leg?"

Phil swung his cast forward to give Nat a better view. "In two months I'll be rehabbing it. In three months I'll be racing again."

Nat nodded, not knowing what to say.

"I wanted to come over and tell you that you did a great job on the course," Phil said hesitantly. "I want to apologize for the hard time I gave you." He gave Nat an embarrassed smile. "Tara explained it was all her fault. I'm still really pissed, but when she told me why. . . . What could I say? I know it wasn't intentional. Anyway, she's going to help me get from class to class, carrying my books and stuff, until my leg is better."

"Yeah," Nat said reluctantly. "Well, I want to . . . you deserve an apology, too. I was wrong. I didn't realize how much work it took to prep a trail. I have a ton more respect now, and understand why you were so worried."

At that moment Tara approached through the crowd.

When Nat saw her, she edged her way over and said, "This Huffy Toss must be a guy thing. I don't get it."

"Looks cool to me," Tara replied.

Nat laughed.

"You've done a great job," Tara told Nat.

Nat smiled. "Thanks."

There was an awkward pause before Tara said, "Well, I'm here like you asked. What do you need me to do?"

"Follow me," Nat replied. She led Tara over to the back of a van. She opened the doors and pulled out a huge plastic garbage bag. "I was hoping you'd police the grounds for litter and empty trash cans." She handed the trash bag to Tara.

"I can do that," Tara said. "In fact, I can do that really well." A look of relief crossed her face. "I would love to pick up trash." She ran off with the trash bag.

Nat returned to the grandstand just in time to watch Kevin come up to the podium to accept the winner's trophy for the Huffy Toss.

Nat screamed and clapped. She was glad Kevin won the toss since she was certain she was going to beat him in the cross-country race.

The gang met by their bikes. When Kevin approached, Wall and Jamil reached in their bags for birthday presents. They handed them to Kevin.

Nat's mouth dropped open. She'd been so wrapped up in the race and the mystery that she had completely forgotten that today was Kevin's birthday.

"I'm so sorry," Nat said, embarrassed. "I totally forgot."

"Not a prob." Kevin shrugged it off. "I know you've been busy."

"I'm really sorry I forgot though," Nat continued. "Is there anything special you want for your birthday?"

Kevin thought for a minute. "No, nothing that I can think of. . . ." He paused.

"Come on," Nat insisted. "Is there anything you want?"

Kevin smiled. "Actually, there is something you can give me and it won't cost you a dime." He clapped Nat on the back. "You can let me win the Bear Claw."

Nat laughed and shook her head. "No way! You've already won the Huffy Toss. That's your birthday present. I'm taking the Bear Claw."

"It's all I want . . . ," Kevin replied.

"ATTENTION BIKERS! ATTENTION BIKERS," the announcer said over the loudspeaker. "THE FIRST EVENT WILL BE THE FOURTEEN-AND-UNDER SPRINT. THIS RACE WILL FEATURE ONE LAP AROUND THE COURSE."

"Come on," Nat called to her friends. "That's us."

The crew ran to their bikes and headed for the start line. Nat and Kevin pushed through the racers to get at the front of the pack. Jamil lingered in the back, while Wall went to the middle.

"Should I leave treads on your face or your back?" Kevin smirked.

"You better wear your shades," Nat answered. "Otherwise, my dust will blind you."

"RACERS! ON YOUR MARK!"

Everyone hopped on their bikes.

"GET SET!"

The sound of pedals ratcheting filled the air.

Bang! The starter pistol went off.

The bikers surged forward like a giant mass of insects. A din of grunts and cries rose from the pack as everyone pushed and pedaled for position.

Nat shot into the lead, climbing a steep hill. She was always a fast starter. Pace yourself, she silently commanded herself. She often burned out early and then had to gut it out at the end.

Kevin fell in behind her and bumped her tire to let her know he was there.

"Back off!" Nat shouted. She bounced over a fallen log and avoided a stump. She put her outside crank down to keep her weight over her tire treads and leaned sharply into the first switchback. She took the shortest, though not necessarily the easiest, line. Barely avoiding a deep rut between two large rocks, she lifted her front tire onto one rock and powered over it.

Nat was in the zone. Her wheels seemed to fly over the ground. She moved down the trail with ease, hardly aware of anything but herself and her bike, until she reached the spot where fresh sawdust was spread loosely across the trail. She automatically braked, though the tree was long gone. Its logs were piled along the side of the trail.

As she passed them, she shifted to a high gear and felt her legs begin to burn. Less than 2K to go, she told herself as she huffed down the rough track to the final sprint along Mack Road.

She was afraid to look, but she felt that Kevin was dropping further back. She couldn't hear his hard breathing as she took a little air when she left the singletrack and entered Mack Road.

Bad move! Worse—chainsuck!

As she landed, she accidentally kicked her derailleur and sent her chain off the sprockets.

"Oops!" Kevin called as he blew past her for the lead.

Nat came quickly to a stop and popped her chain back on. But by now it was too late. She rode across the finish line dead last.

"I hope you appreciate what I just did for you," Nat yelled to Kevin who was being congratulated by the judges.

Kevin smiled. "Yeah, I know. You chainsucked so no one would think you were throwing the race." He walked over to Nat and put his arm around her shoulder. "It's the best birthday present ever!"

biff—to crash

BMX—bicycle motocross; this is a small bike with twenty-inch wheels and one gear; great for doing tricks and catching air

bunny hop—jumping over rocks and small logs by bouncing both wheels into the air at once

catch air—to go flying off a rise and dip

chainsuck—when the chain doubles back on itself in the middle of a gear shift and gets jammed either between the chain rings or between the crank and frame

cross-country—the most popular type of racing for most off-road biking events. A cross-country race goes over hills and through woods

cyclocross—a new kind of race where bikers must traverse all kinds of terrain, sometimes carrying their bike

dab—touching your foot on the ground to keep your balance

dirt biker—a BMX rider

doubletrack—a trail wide enough for two cyclists to ride side by side

downhill—screamingly insane races where riders hurl straight down steep hills; riders usually wear body armor and ride dual suspension bikes

endo—to crash by going over the bike's handlebar. Short for end-over-end

front suspension—shocks on the front fork of a mountain bike to absorb the punishment of the trail

full suspension—shocks on both the front and back of a mountain bike, great for riding downhill, but rough for going uphill since every time the rider cranks his pedal some of the push is absorbed by the rear shock

granny gear—small, lowest gear chain ring, used mainly for climbing

gully—this falls away from the side of the trail

Huffy Toss—a competition where contestants toss an old mountain bike; scores are based on both distance and how many pieces are broken off the bike

off-camber turns—a difficult turn where the trail slopes down on the outside of the curve

pegs—the four-inch metal extensions that stick out the right and left sides of both wheels; they're used to stand on when doing tricks

singletrack—trail so narrow that only one bike can ride through at a time

swag—cool freebies sports manufacturers give away at events

switchback—a ninety-degree or greater turn

technical section—a part of a trail or race course that requires skills other than riding fast. Typically, these parts are singletrack and littered with stumps, rocks, ruts, trees, and other obstacles

thrasher—a daredevil biker, usually a BMX rider

360 tailwhip—biker spins 360 degrees and whips tail 360 degrees as well, while in the air

trail rash—a scrape that happens when you fall and

slide to a stop

washboard—a patch of kidney-bouncing earth ripples

If you're looking for suspense on the slopes, harrowing adventure on the half pipe, or mystery on the trails, look no further!

#1 Deep Powder, Deep Trouble

Jamil must nab a mysterious rogue rider or snowboarding at Hoke Valley will be banned forever.

#2 Crossed Tracks

Who's sabotaging the Bear Claw Mountain bike course? Nat's determined to find out!

#3 Rocked Out: A Summer X Games Special

Kevin and Wall are volunteers at the Summer X Games and become embroiled in a sport-climbing mystery.

#4 Half Pipe Rip-off

Wall needs to track down the graffiti fiend who's framing him for vandalism.

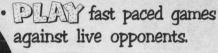